U0143996

伯骏画庐

伯骏画庐作品集

荣宝斋出版社

刘伯骏，笔名老牛骏，1921年生于四川宣汉。1942年考入国立艺术专科学校深造，师从潘天寿、吴茀之、李可染、诸乐三、林风眠诸教授，主攻写意花鸟，兼习指墨。1947年毕业后，潘天寿校长为其在湖州韵海楼举办了"潘天寿门生青年国画家刘伯骏作品展览"。1948年春在国立艺专前任校长陈之佛教授推荐下，与徐悲鸿、李可染、潘天寿、陈之佛等在南京举办了"现代名人书画展"。1949年4月在杭州参加中国人民解放军，在部队从事美术宣传工作。 1949年10月，成为新中国美协第一批会员。1955年从抗美援朝战场转业回到老家大巴山区，潜心探究诗、书、画结合的高境界，执著追求中国画的精气神。1993年中国美协在中国美术馆主办了"刘伯骏书画展"，全国人大副委员长王光英、程思远，全国政协副主席洪学智，原国务院副总理、国防部长张爱萍将军一同为画展剪彩。人民日报、中央电视台、新华社等四十多家省级以上新闻媒体先后作了专题报道。中央电视台《东方之子》《荧屏荟萃》栏目对其作了专访；同年，其作品《朝晖》《夏韵》被中南海收藏。其后谢绝京城各方挽留，回到大巴山潜心创作，作品更有了巨大突破，画界评价：先生的突破对中国画的发展与创新，具有里程碑式的划时代意义；其画作已达入禅之妙境。2004年荣宝斋为其出版了《荣宝斋画谱（168）刘伯骏绘花鸟部分》。2005年中央电视台《大家》栏目播放了对他的专访。2008年4月四川省文联、美协等单位在成都为其主办了"国画大家刘伯骏感恩故乡画展"。2009年"伯骏画庐"在成都奠基。

Born in Xuanhan, Sichuan Province in 1921, Liu Bojun (under the pen name "Old Niujun") was enrolled in National Art Institute and studied under the instruction of professors such as Pan Tianshou, Lin Fengmian, Wu Fuzhi, Li Keran and Zhu Lesan, specializing in freehand bird-and-flower painting and also studying finger painting. After his graduation in 1947, Mr. Pan Tianshou held an exhibition titled Paintings from the Young Artist Liu Bojun for him at Yunhai Building in Huzhou; the next year, an exhibition of contemporary renowned figures featuring masters like Wu Changshuo, Huang Binhong, Zhang Daqian and Chen Zhifo was held in Nanjing, and on the recommendation of Prof. Chen Zhifo, former president of National Art Institute, three of Liu's works also made into the exhibition. In October, 1949, Mr. Liu became one of the first members of China Artists Association. In 1955, he was demobilized from the North Korean War and returned to the Daba Mountains where he devotes himself heart and soul to the exploration of the combination of poetry, calligraphy and painting and the pursuit of the spirit of Chinese painting. In 1993, China Artists Association sponsored his solo exhibition in National Art Museum of china, which was officially opened by Vice Chairmen of National People's Congress, Mr. Wang Guangying and Mr. Cheng Siyuan, Vice Chairman of the CPPCC National Committee, Mr. Hong Xuezhi, and Former Vice Premier of the State Council and Minister of Defense, General Zhang Aiping. This exhibition was reported by more than 40 mainstream newspapers and TV stations such as People's Daily, CCTV and Xinhua News Agency, and CCTV even ran several special features on the event in its programs Oriental Son and TV Guide. In the same year, Mr. Liu was invited to Zhongnanhai and two of his works, Morning Glow and Summer's Charm, entered its art collection. However, later he reclined all the invitations and returned to the Daba Mountains where he avoids all visitors and indulges himself in painting, thus achieving a breakthrough in his works. Professionals remark that Mr. Liu's breakthrough is of epoch-making significance to the development and innovation of Chinese painting, and that his works have achieved the state of profound enlightenment. In 2004, Rongbaozhai Studio published Rongbaozhai Studio's Painting Book No. 168; Bird-and-flower Painting Section by Liu Bojun as the model for Chinese painting. The next year, the CCTV program Master ran several features on him and described him as "a top artist with an unusual life", establishing him as a contemporary master of Chinese painting. In April, 2008, his solo exhibition in Chengdu sponsored by Sichuan Literary Federation and Sichuan Artists Association caused a great sensation among the public. And in 2009, the construction of Bojun's Studio was inaugurated in Chengdu.

大道展雄风　巨笔贯中西
——贺伯骏画庐落成暨《伯骏画庐作品集》首发

文/肖峰

　　欣闻伯骏画庐将于今年"十一"在成都落成，《伯骏画庐》一书也将问世。同时，老兵之恋——国画大家刘伯骏画展，将于2010年九月十五日至十九日在北京中国革命军事博物馆三楼中厅举行。这是我国美术界的一大盛事，我感到无比高兴。

　　刘伯骏同志是我的老学长、老校友，我国艺坛的国画大家，巴山人民的优秀儿子。他脱胎于名门世家，成长于名师名校，锤炼于革命摇篮；他艺术英才早发，自幼聪慧，博学多才，成绩斐然，是我国立艺专学子之佼佼者；他又是革命理想的追求者，抱着一腔爱国情怀，参军参干，屡建殊勋。这样的热血志士是文坛楷模、青年榜样。但在那"左"的年代，"唯成分，唯出身"等精神枷锁，强加在他的头上，致使他的艺术多年被冷落、埋没。这不仅是他个人的不幸，更是祖国美术事业的损失。当然，一位天才的艺术家，由于种种原因，艺途坎坷，在中外美术史上已非罕见。不久前，画界有陈子庄、黄秋园、黄叶树等艺术大家寂寞以终，为世人感叹。去年人们纪念被遗忘的四川山水画大家吴一峰百年诞辰，也是一例。所幸者，伯骏同志得以幸存。晚年，他的艺术得以重放光彩，给他及其艺术以应有的历史评价。

　　伯骏同志的艺术被埋没冷落了近40年，长期得不到重视。生活困厄潦倒，从艺条件艰难，更谈不到社会地位的公允。这些固然是一种不幸，但正是这种不利的客观条件，激发了他主观顽强的奋斗精神。甘于寂寞，默默耕耘，执著地热爱艺术，贴近生活，并从中得到慰藉和力量。从而创造了不朽而独特的艺术，锤炼了高尚的人品。我国数千年的文明史证明，许多先哲圣贤都是从艰苦奋斗中而功成名就的。如文王被囚演《周易》，孔子厄而后写《春秋》，屈原被放逐而作《离骚》，左丘明失明厥有《国语》，司马迁受刑著《史记》。刘伯骏因逆境而艺高。这种奋斗精神是我们中华民族之魂，体现了华夏知识分子的高贵品格。正如藕益大师所言："索不难有才，难有志；不难有志，难有品；不难有品，难有眼。唯有超方眼目，不被时流笼罩者，堪立千古品格，品立则志成，志成才得其所用矣。""有出格见地，方有千古品格；有千古品格，方有超方索问；有超方索问，方有盖世文章。"这段话写照了伯骏同志的人格精神和他对艺术对人生的至精至诚。他淡泊名利、甘守寂寞、素心淡定、宠辱不惊、不尚虚名、不图浮华，心胸开阔，如"海纳百川、有容乃大。壁立千仞，无欲则刚"。因而成就了他的艺术，足以说明"从艺必先立人的道理"。

　　对刘伯骏同志的艺术我不敢妄加评述，从已获得的文献资料及画集中，可领略到这位大家的风采，足以令人肃然起敬。

　　他是巴山之子，名师高徒；学养深厚，博古通今；高风亮节，融入丹青；禅心画意，兼融中西；热血凝诗，丹心铸成；律意墨韵，继往开今；雅俗共赏，推陈出新。

　　一方水土孕育一方人才，巴山蜀水哺育了刘伯骏这位巴山之子。他以"巴山佬"自居，其诗曰："巴山佬，春不倒，挥洒丹青忘年老……欲登巴山临绝顶，淋漓酣畅涂风骚。"抒发着他对故土的热爱。"大巴山的奇峰峻岭，山花野草，不仅给予他无尽的创作素材和灵感；那淳朴的乡风，淡泊的民俗，苦难而憨厚的山民，劳动者那种善良、宽厚、平和、知足、勤劳俭朴的素质，形成了他为人从艺的一颗素心。"对世态炎凉能泰然处之，"不以己悲，不为物喜，倾情画中，如痴如狂"。做到"矢志巴山情高远""杜门静悟似画仙"。这种平民布衣的心境，构成了他作品的主旋律。"平民花"的美人蕉、鸡冠花、向日葵、残荷、野花、蔬果、青菜、萝卜、茄子、辣椒、蘑菇、土豆、苦瓜、红薯、螳螂、壁虎和癞蛤蟆等等都成了他热衷的题材。"问渠哪得清如许，为有源头活水来。"这些题材来自自然，以造化为师。伯骏的艺术之所以感人，正因为他面对现实，不以前人的"程式"所束缚，自成一格，源于生活又高于生活，故气韵生动，充满朝气，具有乡土特色和时代气息，开创了花鸟画的新天地。

"名师出高徒。"他是潘天寿、吴茀之诸师的嫡传弟子，得道于名师的真传。他的艺术力求潘老那种大气磅礴、雄浑奇纵、峥嵘壮阔的气派。更添了些四川的麻辣和巴蜀的泥土气。他师传统，学前人而不泥古落套，总是面向生活"为我所用"，"进得去，又能出得来"。

在手法上，他力求墨韵中具有更强烈的黑白效果，以显示出强悍苍劲和奔放的动感，他的《残荷》《斜风骤雨竹有声》《雪竹》《风竹》《雾竹》画出了与前人不同的境界，正如他所言："有动感才有生命力。古人讲画画要以静制动，我是要以动破静。"开创了花鸟画的一代先河。指画是潘老的绝技，伯骏是其成功传人。

伯骏先生认为，中国画的突破创新首在观念上更新，才能破除传统陈规的藩篱，跟上时代的节奏，因而他的花鸟画从取材章法、笔墨到赋彩，均有系列的革新。传统文人画在构图上讲究空灵，他则不怕布局之"满"；在笔墨上他追求既注重笔意墨韵，又墨不碍色，"色墨合用"，力图吸取恩师林风眠、吴茀先生的赋彩之道。敢于运用西画色彩的对比和色调谐调的效果，有不少成功的尝试。我尤爱《高冠耀眼色灿烂》、《春到巴山》、《鸡冠花》、《独领风骚》、《美人蕉系列》（之一、之三）、《向阳》、《倾国之艳》这几幅画的色彩，精而不妖，鲜而不俗。水、墨、色三者有机融合，意境依然幽雅，恰到好处。林风眠先生与潘天寿先生在继承观点上是有区别的，前者主张"融汇中西"，后者主张"中西要拉开距离"。伯骏同志则居其中，走自己的路。

伯骏虽身处逆境，但笔下的形象充满了朝气，大气磅礴，豪气夺人，蓬勃向上，表达了他丹心报国，肝胆为民的情怀。他是一株"永向着光明的向日葵"，始终向着光明，充满了对国家、对民族、对艺术的挚爱，对生活、对人民、对创作的激情，如八十抒怀诗云："不为陈矩束，画气不画形，对此狂如醉，八十正当春。"他能"活到120岁"，我们愿看到这一天。祝刘老健康长寿，艺术长青！

2010年4月于杭州

（作者系原中国美协副主席、美术报社社长、中国美院院长、著名美术教育家、著名画家）

A Fusion of East and West, A Breakthrough from Conventions (In Celebration of the Opening of Bojun's Painting Studio and the Publication of the Same Titled Book)

Written by Xiao Feng in Hangzhou in April, 2010

The news reaching me of the approaching completion of Bojun's Painting Studio in Chengdu on November 6th this year and the imminent publication of the same titled book by Rongbaozhai Studio, I am very delighted because this would be a prominent event in China's art circles.

Mr. Liu Bojun is an outstanding alumnus of China Academy of Art as well as a great master of Chinese painting. Brought up in a family of scholars and imparted education at such a famous art academy, he demonstrated brilliant talent at an early age,learned from various people and various schools, and achieved excellent results, thus making himself a top student among his peers. However, in those left-wing years, Mr. Liu was held back by his political background; as a result, his art talent was neglected and suppressed for years,which is not only the misfortune of Mr. Liu himself but also a loss of China's art circles. Of course, it is not uncommon whether in China or abroad that a talented artist should suffer from hardship in his career due to certain reasons. Not long ago, Chen Zizhuang, Huang Qiuyuan and Huang Yeshu, all of whom are great masters in the art world, passed away in obscurity, evoking a feeling of lament in people. Another example is a couple of years ago people's commemoration of the centenary of Wu Yifeng, a Sichuanese master of landscape painting who was left out of public sight. Fortunately, Mr. Liu's paintings are able to reach and impress the public in his later years. It is high time the art world gave Mr. Liu and his works the historical evaluation they well deserve.

Neglected and suppressed for nearly four decades, Mr. Liu's art talent was for a long time not taken seriously;during that time, he suffered from difficulties in pursuing his art creation, let alone winning the social status he should deserve. This is no doubt a misfortune, but it is just these adversities and hardships that evoked his persistence and fighting spirit with which he was willing to live with solitude and devote himself to painting, persistently pursuing the highest level of art. He stays close to real life, from which he derives consolation and strength, thus allowing him to create immortal and unique paintings and develop noble quality of both his works and himself. The thousands-of-years-long civilization of our nation proves the fact that many great figures rise to accomplishments from distress. For example, King Wen of Zhou wrote Book of Changes in imprisonment; Confucius wrote Spring and Autumn Annals in adversity; Qu Yuan's Li Sao was born in exile; Tso Ch'iuming composed Discourses of the States in blindness; and Sima Qian was provoked by his castration and composed The Records of the Grand Historian. Similarly, Mr. Liu acquired exceptional painting skills in overcoming hardship. This unyielding spirit is just the soul of the Chinese people. As Great Master Ouyi says: It is true that talent is easier to acquire than ambition; ambition is easier to acquire than morality; and morality is easier to acquire than insight. Only those who are with such detached insight and not blinded by the contemporary tide can develop a rare quality which is the prerequisite of ambition which is the prerequisite of talent. He also says: Exceptional judgment precedes rare qualities; rare qualities precede preeminent knowledge; preeminent knowledge precedes unparalleled writings. These words act as a mirror of Mr. Liu's qualities and spirit as well as his absolute sincerity toward art and life. Indifferent to wealth and fame and devoted to a simple, peaceful life, Mr. Liu is never moved by honor or disgrace, and always keeps an open mind to the world,just as the saying describes, "The sea admits hundreds of rivers for its capacity to hold; the cliff rises a thousand feet sheer for its strength of desirelessness." All these reveal the truth that great personalities precede great works.

It would be presumptuous of me to comment on Mr. Liu's works, but existing literature and his paintings give me a taste of the master's brilliance which easily inspires awe and admiration in me. Learning from both the past and the present and adding his own personalities into his paintings, he has achieved a fusion of East and West and a breakthrough from old conventions.

The natural beauty of Sichuan brings up Liu who calls himself "Old Liu of the Ba Mountain" and even writes a poem to express his love of the place which reads: I am the son of the Ba Mountain; splashing ink my age have I forgotten. I will ascend the crest of the Ba Mountain; and paint to my heart's content. This poem expresses his love for the land. "The hills and trees of the Daba Mountain provide him with endless objects and inspiration for his paintings; the goodness, simplicity, diligence and peacefulness of its people help him develop purity of mind both as a person and as an artist." He takes external affiars calmly and peacefully. As one of his poems reads: Not saddened by personal losses; not pleased by external gains. I immerge myself into painting; like a crazy man in love. He also writes lines like "committed to the Ba Mountain but aiming high" and "locking myself up behind the door and reveling in the wonder of painting". This civilian state of mind constitues the main theme of his paintings. In his paintings there is the vivid representation of commonplace objects such as cannas, cockscomb flowers, sunflowers, withering lotuses, wild flowers, vegetables and fruits, turnips, eggplants, peppers, mushrooms and potatoes, bitter gourds and sweet potatoes, matises and lizzards. "How can it be so clear and cool? For water fresh comes from its source." These objects come from nature and ordinary life. Mr. Liu's paintings are so touching because he deals with real life, refuses to be confined to past patterns and establishes his own unique style. The closeness to and detachment from real life makes his works full of life and vitality and bear the characteristics of the countryside and of the contemporary world, marking a new phase of bird-and-flower painting.

A great teacher produces a brilliant student. Inheriting from great masters such as Pan Tianshou and Wu Fuzhi, Mr. Liu represents in his paintings the combination of Pan Tianshou's imposing vigor, Lin Fengmian's comprehensive employment of wash, ink and color, Li Keran's sketching of nature, Wu Fuzhi's richness of variation, and the authentic natural beauty of Sichuan. He learns from traditions but is not confined to them.

As for techniques, Mr. Liu seeks to achieve a more intense contrast between black and white in the tones to better convey the imposing vigor and wild motion. For example, his Withering Lotuses, Bamboos in a Sudden Downpour, Bamboos in Snow, Bamboos in Wind and Bamboos in Mist deliver an image of overwhelming forcefulness and different from that of his predecessors. As he said, "Motion brings life to paintings. Painters in the past emphasized stillness over motion, but I employ motion to replace stillness." In this way, Mr. Liu begins a new phase of freehand bird-and-flower painting. Mr. Pan Tianshou's finger painting is a matchless feat, and Mr.Liu is considered his successor.

Mr. Liu believes that the breakthrough in Chinese painting can only materialize through the innovation in conception to break away from old conventions and catch up with the contemporary world. Therefore, there are a series of breakthroughs and innovations in the objects, composition, tones and coloring in his paintings. Traditional artists attach great importance to the reservation of vacant space in composition, while Mr. Liu is not afraid to make "full" use of the paper; he emphasizes the tones of the ink and at the same time supplements them with the colors of paint. His adoption of the coloring skills of Lin Fengmian and Wu Fuzhi and bold employment of the contrast and balance of colors in Western paintings produce several successful works. My favorite paintings are his Brilliant Corollas, Spring Visits the Ba Mountain, Cockscomb Flowers, Taking the Lead, The Cannas Series, Toward the Sun, and Overwhelming Beauty. In these paintings, the colors are exquisite but not sensual, bright but not vulgar, and the effective combination of wash, ink and color creates exactly an elegant image. In fact, Mr. Lin Fengmian and Mr. Pan Tianshou hold opposite views toward Chinese painting, the former advocating the fusion of the Eastern and the Western styles while the later insisting on the reservation of their differences. Mr. Liu takes the road in between and has formed his own style.

Mr. Liu has suffered from adversity, but the objects in his works are always permeated with life, vigor and prosperity. He is just like a sunflower, always looking at the bright side of life and expressing his deep love of the country, the people and art and his passion for painting. One of his peoms reads: From the rigid rules have I broken loose; resemblence in spirit not in form is what I chase. With painting have I fallen crazily in love; though eighty years old, I am still in the prime of my life. He vows to continue painting till 120 years old, and we may that his dream come true and his art survive time. I hope that Bojun's Art Studio would descend through generations.

About the Author:
Xiao Feng is the Vice President of China Artists Association, the former President of China Academy of Art, the President of China Art Weekly and a famed art educator and critic.

目录

Contents

日当午
97cm×180cm

At Noon
97cm×180cm

无畏骄阳困
68cm×68cm

Fearing Not the Blazing Sun
68cm×68cm

日午羞高阳
68cm×68cm

Outshining the Midday Sun
68cm×68cm

追日
68cm×68cm

Chasing the Sun
68cm×68cm

吻天
68cm×68cm

Kissing the Sky
68cm×68cm

向日葵
68cm×68cm

Sunflowers
68cm×68cm

山风唱和向阳开
180cm×97cm

Sunflowers Bloomingin the
Wind Toward the Sun
180cm×97cm

昂首挺立向阳开
68cm×68cm

Sunflowers Blooming Proudly Toward the Sun
68cm×68cm

和祥
68cm×68cm

Peaceful Harmony
68cm×68cm

嫣红绿正肥
68cm×68cm

A Colorful Scene
68cm×68cm

花笑放清香
68cm×68cm

Blooming Aroma
68cm×68cm

舞
97cm×180cm

Dance! Dance! Dance!
97cm×180cm

飞笔走线荷鲜花
68cm×68cm

The Painting of Lotuses
68cm×68cm

鱼乐图
68cm×68cm

Fish Paradise
68cm×68cm

秋色
97cm×180cm

Autumn Charm
97cm×180cm

留得枯荷听雨声
68cm×136cm

Withered Lotuses and the Sound of Rain
68cm×136cm

巴山夫民八六年夏书于成都方锦
己四赵前阳光灿烂窗
雍雅制古笑鱼坐雨声

19

斜风骤雨竹有声
97cm×180cm

Bamboos in the Storm
97cm×180cm

雨霁
136cm×68cm

After the Rain
136cm×68cm

春风
97cm×90cm

Spring Breeze
97cm×90cm

朝晖
97cm×180cm

Morning Glow
97cm×180cm

竹韵
97cm×90cm

Beauty of the Bamboos
97cm×90cm

瑞雪
100cm×68cm

Auspicious Snow
100cm×68cm

叶儿飘
68cm×136cm

Falling Leaves
68cm×136cm

天龙图
68cm×136cm

Dragon in the Sky
68cm×136cm

闹春
97cm×93m

Alive in Spring
97cm×93cm

喜盈春
68cm×68cm

Spring Filled with Happiness
68cm×68cm

雪里香
98cm×68cm

Sweet Scent in
the Snow
98cm×68cm

老梅怒放新枝生
180cm×97cm

Old Plum Tree Bursting
with New Blossoms
180cm×97cm

铁骨丹心
97cm×90cm

Muscles of Iron, Heart of Gold
97cm×90cm

争春
97cm×180cm

Vying for Favor in Spring
97cm×180cm

梅魂日永

二〇〇七
年
乙亥
初春
巴山花光片
光華片
莲十六
寺道州丁
郭若鐵山
老梅歸身
張修揮酒
買楼米
争畫圖
蘭竹前
开花日

37

闹春
180cm×97cm

Celerating the
Advent of Spring
180cm×97cm

弄春
68cm×68cm

Full Blooming in Spring
68cm×68cm

竞争春
180cm×97cm

Competing for
Favor in Spring
180cm×97cm

愈老愈精神
97cm×90cm

The Older, The More Vigorous
97cm×90cm

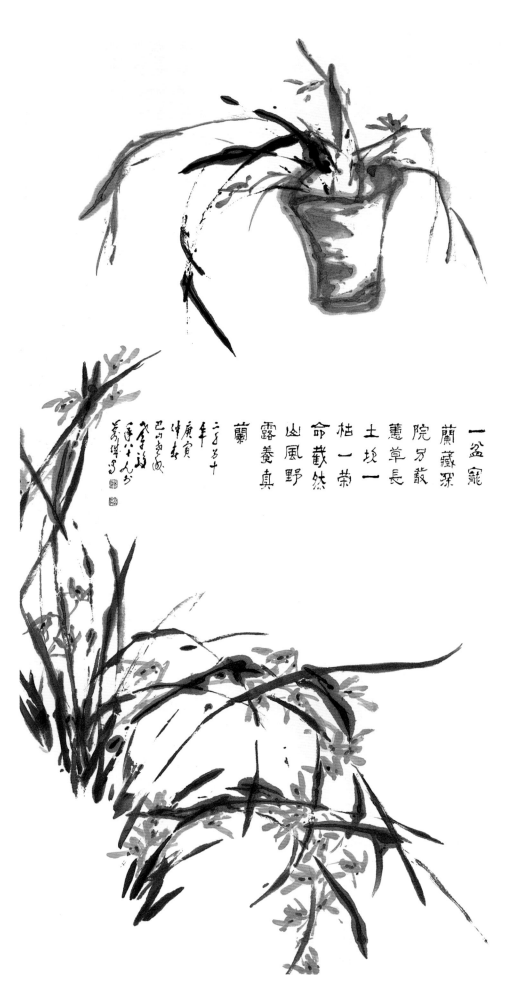

一盆寵蘭藏深
院另散蕙草長
土坂一枯一榮
命截然幽風野
露養真蘭

二子之十年庚寅仲春巴山雨之叟於李明運十九好蒙祥写

山风野露养真兰
136cm×68cm

Genuine Orchids
Grown in Wild Nature
136cm×68cm

春风吹绿舞
136cm×68cm

Green LeavesDancing
to the Spring Breeze
136cm×68cm

好与春风舞蕙兰
68.5cm×72.5cm

Orchids Dancing to the Spring Breeze
68.5cm×72.5cm

香入千万家
68cm×68cm

Releasing Aroma into
Surrounding Households
68cm×68cm

沐山风野露
97cm×180cm

Bathed in Nature
97cm×180cm

喜沐晨光着春装
68cm×136cm

Bathed in the
Spring Morning Sun
68cm×136cm

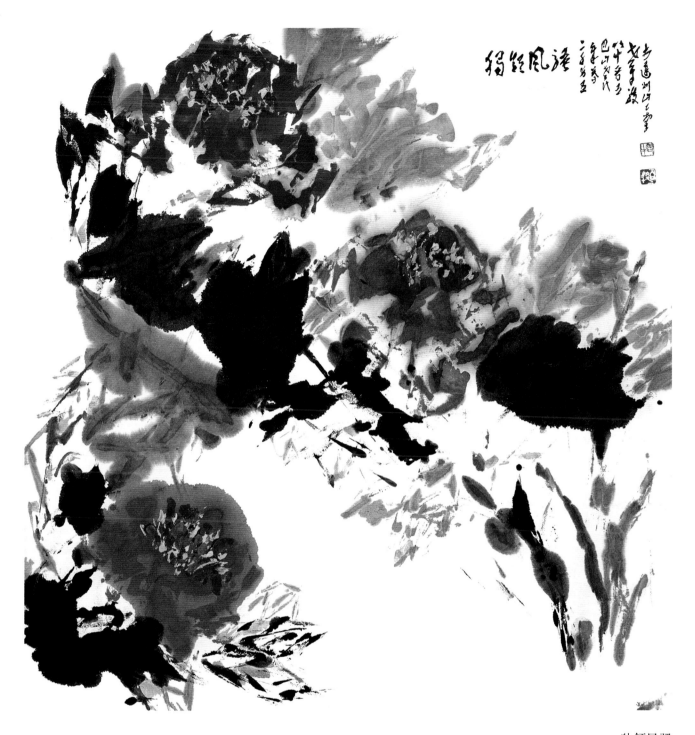

独领风骚
68cm×68cm

Taking the Lead
68cm×68cm

天香
53cm×136cm

Divine Beauty
53cm×136cm

天香人和
68cm×136cm

Divine Beauty, Peaceful Harmony
68cm×136cm

天娇系列之一
68cm×68cm

Heavenly Charm Series I
68cm×68cm

天娇系列之二
68cm×136cm

Heavenly Charm Series II
68cm×136cm

天娇系列之四
68cm×68cm

Heavenly Charm Series IV
68cm×68cm

天娇系列之三
70cm×51cm

Heavenly Charm Series III
70cm×51cm

墨牡丹
68cm×68cm

Peonies in Ink
68cm×68cm

醉墨香
97cm×68cm

Intoxicated by
the Scent of Ink
97cm×68cm

59

新放
76cm×112cm

New Blossoms
76cm×112cm

无畏风雨袭
68cm×68cm

Fearing Not the Storm
68cm×68cm

日中天
68cm×68cm

Midday
68cm×68cm

醉美
68cm×136cm

Mesmerizing Beauty
68cm×136cm

美人蕉系列之一
97cm×90cm

Cannas Series 1
97cm×90cm

美人蕉系列之二
97cm×90cm

Cannas Series II
97cm×90cm

美人蕉系列之三
97cm×90cm

Cannas Series III
97cm×90cm

怒放
97cm×90cm

In Full Bloom
97cm×90cm

朝霞相映愈增辉
68cm×136cm

Morning Sunglow Shines Down
68cm×136cm

老林
69cm×121cm

Old Woods
69cm×121cm

绿藏娇
68cm×68cm

Pretty Flowers Hidden Among Thick Green Foliage
68cm×68cm

高冠争妍华
68cm×68cm

Colorful Corollas Sun
68cm×68cm

小憩
136cm×68cm

A Little Res
136cm×68cm

74

后记

　　我自五岁习画，今逾八十五载矣。虽历经风雨坎坷，仍一日不曾搁笔。实未想扬名立万，独醉心绘画乐趣。难言画有所成，亦常怀感恩之心。从自幼手把手教我作画的父母叔舅和给我启蒙的川东名画家黎见三老师，到国立艺专诸恩师，以及丹青同道，皆予我携扶激励。值此画册出版之际，谨表达由衷的感恩之情。

　　我首先要感谢荣宝斋出版社的编辑同志为本书出版所付出的心血。

　　我要特别感谢前人民日报总编辑、九届全国人大常委、教科文卫委员会副主任委员范敬宜先生为"伯骏画庐"赐题。

　　我还要特别感谢前中国美术家协会副主席、中国美术学院院长、《美术报》社长肖锋先生在百忙之中为本书作序。同时我要感谢前中国美术家协会常务副主席、党组书记王琦先生，老战友洪炉先生对本书出版的关心和帮助。

　　我还要感谢我的家人对我生活的悉心照顾，感谢泳村、御力、贞文、慧明等为筹建"伯骏画庐"所做的一切。

刘伯骏
2010年7月于锦城锦江之畔

图书在版编目（ＣＩＰ）数据

伯骏画庐作品集 / 刘伯骏绘． —— 北京 ：荣宝斋出
版社，2010.9
ISBN 978-7-5003-1210-9
Ⅰ．①伯… Ⅱ．①刘… Ⅲ．①中国画－作品集－中
国－当代 Ⅳ．①J222.7
中国版本图书馆CIP数据核字(2010)第146600号

策　　划：向荣高　羊慧明　刘南平
翻　　译：李笑梅
责任编辑：孙志华
装帧设计：李娟
审　　读：江金照
责任校对：王桂荷
责任印制：孙行　毕景滨

伯骏画庐作品集

出版发行：荣宝斋出版社
地　　址：北京市宣武区琉璃厂西街19号
邮政编码：100052
制　　版：北京三益印刷有限公司
印　　刷：北京燕泰美术制版印刷有限公司

开　本：889毫米×1194毫米　1/16
印　张：5.5
版　次：2010年9月第1版
印　次：2010年9月第1次印刷
印　数：0001-2000
定　价：128.00元